CHOSEN BY THE GRIZZLY

OBSESSED MOUNTAIN MATES

ARIANA HAWKES

Imprint: Independently published

ISBN: 9798859392711

Cover art: Thunderface Design

www.arianahawkes.com

Callie

"*L*et me guess." My best friend Monica bounds up the stairs behind me. "A weekend in a humongously expensive spa?"

"Nope."

"Bunny ears and bride squad T-shirts in Las Vegas? Getting wasted in New Orleans?

A sailing trip around the Caribbean islands?"

"Nope, nope and nope." I throw open my bedroom door.

I hear Monica's intake of breath, then she pushes past me and stares at my bed. It's piled high with all kinds of stuff. I have no idea what most of it is.

"Whoa! Are my eyes deceiving me, or is this *hiking gear*?" When she spins to face me, her face is such a picture of confusion, I burst out laughing.

"I wish they were, trust me. But no, my older sister has decided to spend her bachelorette weekend long-distance hiking."

"Wow." Monica picks up a can of bear spray and examines the label. "I wouldn't have guessed Lindsay was big on the *great outdoors*."

I smirk at the hitch in her voice. She never says anything bitchy. She doesn't need to. She can put a ton of snark into the arch of an eyebrow. "That's the kicker. She's even more un-outdoorsy than me. But this is how she wanted to spend her bachelorette. Going on a three-day trip into the wilderness with her three closest friends. And me."

"Who else is coming?"

"Ashley, Brittany, and…" I stare into space. My sister's friends are so alike, I often confuse them. "And Madison—"

"Madison? The one with the fingernails?"

I giggle. "Yup."

"I wonder how those talons are gonna cope with a bunch of guy ropes."

"Oh, we're staying in huts or something. Think tents would be a step too far."

Monica narrows her eyes. "I think your sister is up to something."

"I'm not gonna lie, the thought had crossed my mind, too." Being *up to something* is my sister's modus operandi. But it usually involves buying fake followers for her Insta account, or bullying hard-working busi-nesses into giving her free swag in exchange for "exposure".

"What, though? I looked at the online map already. There's nothing out there. It's literally just wilderness, with a few tourist huts scattered here and there."

"Hmm. And Lindsay has planned the route?"

"Yup." She might not be outdoorsy, but she's sure resourceful, my sister. And when she wants something, nothing will stop her from getting it. Like her fiancé, for example. He had a scholarship to a really good school, but suddenly, he decided he wasn't going to take it, and he wound up going to community college with Lindsay instead. Her dream is to become a full-time influencer. Honestly, there couldn't be a better job for her.

"Interesting. Very interesting," Monica mutters thoughtfully.

"This is going to suck big hairy elephant balls." I stare down at the backpack I just bought with real, undiluted hatred. It's already full, and there's still so much that needs to go in it.

"It might, but it's just three days," Monica says. "Then you'll be back, and we'll go see Dead Fox Parade together."

I throw her a grateful smile. "That's literally the one thing that's keeping me going." I slump down on my bed. "But three whole days with my sister and her best buds. With no way of escaping…" I trail off. My brain is still not capable of processing just how bad this is gonna be.

"Hey, if they drive you crazy, you can just… take off by yourself." She wiggles her eyebrows ironically. "Just like in the movies. What could possibly go wrong?"

"Don't. You think I haven't already imagined what it

would be like to be attacked by a grizzly?" I try to stuff a sweater into my backpack, but it's no good. With an epic groan, I haul everything out and start to repack. Suddenly I'm close to tears. "I can't do this..." I blurt out. "Her friends are so mean and bitchy, and they all look down on me because I'm studying childcare, and I'm not thin and pretty and I've never had a boyfriend."

Or even been kissed. But luckily, they don't know that.

Monica grabs my hands and fixes me with a stern look. "Listen to me, Callie. You're more beautiful, inside and out, than all four of them put together. You're as funny as hell, and you don't have fake lips, or tits, or ass cheeks..."

I giggle. "Okay, that last bit is true."

"This probably isn't going to rank as one of the greatest weekends of all time. But it's only three days, and you're doing your sister a solid, just by being there and making sure they don't all take themselves out through some stunning act of stupidity."

"Thanks, Mon, you're right," I say. "It's just three days."

"That's the spirit, girl. You repeat that like a mantra."

Just three days.

Trouble is, if I know my big sister as well as I think I do, a lot can happen in three days.

"My feet fricking hurt." Madison leans against a tree, pulls off her glittery pink sneaker and examines an angry-looking blister on her heel.

I heave off my backpack and dump it on the ground, then I root around until I find what I'm looking for. "Blister bandage." I hand over the little flesh-colored disc without further comment.

"Thanks," Madison says grudgingly, and almost snatches it out of my hand. She curled her lip at my sensible trail shoes and hiking pants this morning, but I'm gonna do my best to forget about that now.

I perch on a tree stump and wipe my glasses on my Dry Fit T-shirt. It's a relief to take the weight off for a moment. I'm hot, sweaty, and my back is aching like crazy. This morning, Lindsay surprised us by arriving with two tents. Apparently, we'll need to camp out on the first night, because there's no hut close to our first stop. Kinda begs the question of why we're stopping there at all. But hey, I don't make the decisions around here.

Anyway, in true Lindsay style, she concealed this piece of information until it was too late for us to back out. *It'll be fun*, she said. *They're not heavy, either! We can take it in turns to carry them.*

Of course, that didn't happen. The other three are carrying small, fashion backpacks. I've got a suspicion they're full of make-up, wilderness non-appropriate clothing, and not much else. They also don't have straps for attaching tents, et cetera. So, Lindsay and I have wound up carrying the tents the whole time.

"How much farther?" Ashley whines, fluffing her curly blonde hair around her shoulders. She's been struggling the most, so far. She's rail thin, but she's been puffing hard on the uphill sections, and she seems so out of shape I'm kind of worried for her.

My sister slides her phone out of her back pocket. Like the others, she's in full make-up, including false eyelashes, but at least she's wearing trail shoes and sensible shorts and a tanktop. "We'll be there in another hour," she says.

"An hour?!" Brittany seethes. "You didn't say we'd be walking so far each day, Linz."

"We're only going ten miles," my sister replies airily. "It'll be worth it, you'll see."

I roll my eyes. Spending the night in a basic campsite doesn't seem like a great prize after a whole day's walking and bitching and complaining.

But Lindsay is real upbeat. Like, I don't think I've ever seen her so *pumped* before. From the moment we gathered in the forest parking lot this morning, she seemed like she could hardly wait to get to our destination.

The other three were also excited at first, but before we'd even gone a mile, their good moods had been replaced by constant complaints.

As for me, funnily, I'm actually enjoying the hiking part. I offered to bring up the rear, but that was mainly so I could drop back and put some distance between myself and the others. And it's kinda cool being in the forest, far from civilization. The air smells so fresh and alive. And if I tune out the mean girls' whining, I hear nothing but bird song and the rustling of little animals in the undergrowth. Who'da thunk it?

Maybe I'll come back here someday. See if Monica

wants to come with me. I snap a selfie and send it to her. There's not a lot of Internet connection out here, but eventually a pair of blue ticks appear next to it.

You got this! she replies right away, with a thumbs-up and starry eyes.

She's such a sweetheart, and I'm so lucky she's my bestie. My parents weren't around a lot when I was growing up. They got divorced when I was young, and they both seemed more interested in their new families. Lindsay was also less of a support than I needed. But Monica has been there for me through thick and thin.

When Madison's laced her sneakers up and everyone's sipped their diet sodas, we set off again.

The last hour is the worst. The sun is dropping lower in the sky, casting the forest in an eerie gloom. It'll suck if it's already dark when we arrive. My feet get heavier with every step and the skin on my shoulders is being rubbed raw.

"We're here!" Lindsay exclaims from the front of the line at last.

I emerge from the trail into a clearing. And *stare*. I'm in an open space, about twenty yards across, surrounded by a bunch of tall, sinister-looking pines. There's a hollow in the middle of it that might be a firepit, but that's all.

"This is it?" I demand.

Uncertainty flickers in Lindsay's eyes, but then she clasps her hands and exclaims in her loud, chipper voice, "isn't this *great*? Just me and my best girlfriends, out in nature."

My frustration and exhaustion roll into a big ball of anger.

"Lindsay, we could've gotten the same effect if we'd camped right by the parking lot. What the hell are we doing out here?"

"Don't be such a party-pooper, Callie. We're getting back to basics." She eases her backpack off her shoulders and it hits the ground with a thunk. "Disconnecting." She pulls out her phone. "C'mon. Selfie."

Instantly, the other three quit looking bedraggled, and they rush over to Lindsay, shoving their tits toward the camera and grinning like they're having the best day of their entire lives.

Remember the mantra, I tell myself: *In less than three days, this will all be over.*

But, by the time I've joined then, Lindsay has already snapped the photo, and she's shoving her phone back in her pocket.

"Don't worry, Callz, there'll be other opportunities later," she tells me, in that patronizing tone of hers that makes me want to slap her.

Whatever.

"We'd better put the tents up before it gets dark," I say. I pull my tent out of its bag and lay it on the ground. Earlier today, I downloaded some step-by-step instructions on how to put it up. Doesn't look too hard. At least, it wouldn't be if I wasn't so darn tired right now.

"Wanna give me a hand, Madison?" I call, since she's nearest. But she wanders away from me, occupied with something very important on her phone.

Okay. Like I always say, I'm not a team player. I work best by myself.

TEN MINUTES LATER, I'm... done. I stare at my tent in amazement. It's perfectly upright. All the ropes are connected to all the pegs. When I give it a shove, it bounces right back. It looks like it might even survive some inclement weather. I walk around it slowly. So *this* is how camping works. It's a portable little home, out in the wilderness. Kinda awesome. I feel a little bit proud of myself. With more enthusiasm than I've felt on the trip so far, I start hauling my stuff out of my backpack and arranging it inside the tent. I lay out my sleeping bag and inflatable pillow, then check my portable lantern is working. Honestly, it's so darn cozy in here. I've got a bag of trail mix and a packet of deer jerky. I could just zip the flaps shut, have a little solo dinner, and fall asleep reading my Kindle—

"Argghh!" A high-pitched scream breaks through my reverie.

I burst out of the tent, eyes darting everywhere.

In the middle of the clearing, Ashley is doing a manic dance, skinny limbs thrashing while she shrieks and slaps herself all over.

"Is she having a seizure?" I yell, charging toward her, arms outstretched. I'm not sure what I'm planning to do. But I've gotta do *something*. Everyone else is just standing around, watching.

"Fucking mosquitoes!" Ashley squeals.

Ohh. I plant my hands on my hips and burst out laughing.

"It's not funny, goddamnit. They're eating me alive!"

I dart back to my tent, grab my can of Cutter Backwoods and start spraying. I'm barely done blasting Ashley, when Brittany grabs it out of my hand and douses her legs with it.

"You should wear long pants and a long-sleeved shirt in the evenings," I say, eyeing four sets of bare, fake-tanned limbs. "This is when mosquitoes are most active."

"Huh? Oh—" Madison looks down at her skimpy outfit, then curls her lip at me. "Well, I guess I didn't bring any *long-sleeved shirts.*" She imitates me in a tight-assed voice.

I shrug. "Get eaten alive then. See if I give a crap."

I stalk over to Lindsay. She's wrestling with the other tent. "Let me help," I tell her. She steps back with a shrug, and I get to work.

In a few more minutes, I'm done. A large, yellow tent is standing on the opposite side of the clearing from mine.

"Thanks, sis," she says in an artificially bright voice.

I slide her a suspicious glance. She's definitely up to something. Every last one of them hates being here, but they still seem kinda pumped. They keep showing each other their phone screens and whispering excitably about some dude called Jason Trentino, whoever he is.

Whatever. As long as I've done my sisterly duty, I'm good.

Right now, I need to get some water before it gets

dark. I also need to get away from these airheads for a while. I grab my water bottle, purifier and a quick-dry towel and stalk out of the clearing.

According to my maps app, there's a stream nearby. I orient myself and start walking. The trees are dense here, and it's getting dark. I stumble through the undergrowth, praying nothing sinks its fangs into my legs. My attention darts between the endless trees and the little blue arrow on my glowing phone screen.

I feel a little shaky and my heart is beating faster than usual. It's pretty darn scary being out in the wilderness like this, totally alone. There's no phone signal. My maps app is only working because I downloaded it earlier. If my phone suddenly malfunctioned right now, I'd be screwed. I don't think I'd be able to make it back to the campsite by myself.

But that's not gonna happen. The battery is nearly full, and I've got a portable charger as well.

And here's the stream. When I hear the sound of running water, I let out a long breath. It's real pretty. Crystal clear and tinkling over soft gray stones. I crouch down at the water's edge and fill up my purifier. It's also freezing cold. *Damn.* I was planning to have a little alfresco wash. I mean, there are only four people who are going to smell me, and I've long given up on caring what they think, but it's nice to be clean. Okay, here goes.

I strip off my clothes, step in the freezing flow and duck right down.

Sheesh. I literally have to clap a hand over my mouth to stop myself from screaming.

But after a few seconds, I stop feeling cold, and the water is actually *refreshing*. Kinda silky. I work fast, scrubbing all the day's dirt away, then I reach for the towel—

What was that? My head snaps up.

A rustle in the trees, on the far side of the stream. I peer into the gathering gloom. Did something move? My old schoolteacher used to tell us things look weird at twilight. Sometimes you see shapes that don't exist—

What the hell?

Okay, *that* definitely exists.

There's a cabin in the distance. It's half-hidden by trees, but it's right there, no question. I can clearly make out a wooden front door and a square window with four little panes of glass. There's even a little porch. What the actual fuck? Here we are in one of the most isolated places on the planet, and I'm looking at someone's home. Somebody lives here. Suddenly, my throat feels tight and my heart is beating like crazy.

Something isn't right here.

I scramble out of the water, haul my wet clothes on, and *run like hell*.

2

Jason

*M*y beast comes to a dead stop, ten feet from my cabin. It raises its snout to the evening air and sniffs hard.

Humans. A scent I haven't smelled for a long, long time, but it's unmistakable.

Fury rolls through me.

What the hell are they doing here? I've built this place deep in the wilderness, where no one could find me. If it was any more isolated, it'd be on the fucking moon. There are no active trails leading here. There was an old campsite a few hundred yards away, but it's long been abandoned. It doesn't even show up on any maps apps anymore. I've made darn sure of that.

Bristling with annoyance, I follow the scent toward

the stream. I splash through the water and stop again on the far bank.

It's stronger here. And it's not the scent of many humans, but one.

One female.

And she smells good. More than good.

A sweet, delicate smell, like the first snowdrop of the year rolls through me.

My beast snuffles at the ground, desperate to know more about her.

She stood here on this spot for a little while.

Her hair is freshly shampooed, and it's lustrous and healthy.

There's a light scent of fresh perspiration—she's been working hard today.

Her skin smells like cherry blossom.

She's young, no more than twenty-five, and… Something roars through my veins. Something hot and hungry and urgent…

She's unmated.

I inhale again and again, filling my lungs with her intoxicating virgin scent.

But what's that? A sharper tang of fear. I frown. She's afraid of this forest? I don't blame her. It's no place for a human. What is she doing out here all by herself?

I shouldn't care. What I should do is go after her, show her my teeth and claws and make darn sure she never thinks about coming back here again.

But the thought of her fear is like a knife in my gut. I don't want to scare her any more than she is already.

I'll just go back to my cabin, pretend I imagined

that delicious waft of virgin scent. Maybe I did. I snicker to myself. Five years alone in the wilderness, and a whole lifetime without a mate, and I'm getting olfactory hallucinations. That's real fucked up, Trentino.

No, I didn't imagine it. My beast doesn't *imagine* stuff. It *reacts*. And right now, it's all but electrified with need. All it can think about is tracking this female down, and putting a claim on her.

Shit. I've never felt this way before. But now it's happening. My animal has awakened. My blood is flowing hot in my veins, and my cock is pulsing like a heat-seeking missile.

Before I know what I'm doing, my beast is following this heady feminine scent into the trees.

Can't hurt to see what she looks like, I guess. I'll just take a quick look at her, then I'll go back to my cabin, and jerk off before my balls explode.

The tang of her fear gets more and more dominant with every step. She's heading toward the old campsite. There's a flicker of orange light in the distance. She's started a campfire for herself? Smart girl.

I make sure to walk silently. I might weigh 700 pounds, but like any bear, I can be light on my feet when I need to be.

I'm not far away now. My heart swells with every step, and my whole body buzzes with anticipation. I reach the end of the path and the clearing opens up.

I direct my gaze to the campfire eagerly.

She's not alone. The air is full of a sickly artificial flower odor, and I make out three, four five figures. All human females. Damn. I should've been prepared for this.

They're all standing close together. So, which one is she? I look from one to the other, to the other.

When I zero in on the one who's crouching down in front of the fire, my heart bangs against my ribcage.

That one.

Of course.

There's no doubt. How could there be?

Mate, my bear purrs.

I let out a long sigh. She's the one. Didn't I know it the moment I picked up her scent for the very first time?

As she stirs a spoon in a pan, I watch her, fixated. Burning to take in every little bit of her.

She has long, curly dark hair, which is hanging down like a curtain, obscuring her features. She's dressed in practical hiking gear, but there's no concealing her killer curves. My mouth waters as I stare at her full, round tits straining beneath the white fabric of her shirt. When she dusts off her hands and stands up, I'm treated to the sight of curvy hips and a full, round ass.

And, glory of fucking glories, she turns her head in my direction, and I see her face for the first time. She's wearing glasses, which frame a pair of huge hazel eyes. She has a small, snub nose with a scattering of freckles, and sweet, cherry-shaped pink lips. She also has the cutest dimples in her cheeks. My chest aches. She's the most beautiful thing I've seen in my life.

As I gaze at her, mesmerized, she tilts her head to the side. My breath catches. I could swear she's looking directly at me. But that's impossible. Human eyesight isn't that sharp. And it's dark. She frowns, removes her glasses, rubs them on her shirt and puts them on again. She keeps on staring into the trees, then she takes a step toward me. My heart jumps into my throat. She can't have seen me. But does she sense something? Does she know her mate is here—?

"Callie!" one of the others calls. Her eyebrows draw together, as if in annoyance. Then she turns a one-eighty and returns to the group.

I close my eyes.

Callie.

My mate's name.

It rolls through me like honey. I growl it out, over and over again. And then I imagine those sweet cherry lips calling out my name as I drive her wild with ecstasy.

Jason, don't stop...

Jason, please...

Yes, she's going to cry my name, while I drive her wild. Make her come all over my dick.

Fuck. I'm so hard for her already, and I haven't even spoken to her yet. I can't wait to meet her, to learn all about her. Find out what she's doing here, in the middle of the wilderness.

My beast is poised, muscles burning with pent-up energy. It's desperate to run to her. But I can't approach her like this. I'll scare the hell out of her.

I'll just stay here for a little bit. Watch her. See what I can find out about her.

I stay in the shadows and prick up my ears.

Although, my damn heart is beating so hard, I can hardly hear anything over it.

She crouches down again, stirring something in a pot. Beans and Franks. What passes for human food in the wilderness. I'll go hunt her a rabbit instead. Gut it, portion it, then lay it out for them. Create a diversion or something, so they don't see me doing it.

The idea surges in my beast's brain, and it prepares to dash into the forest, nostrils already picking up the scent of wild rabbit.

No, doofus. I rein it back in.

Five human women, alone in the forest? It won't look like dinner; it'll look like a mutilated corpse, put there by a psychotic stalker.

She's working hard, preparing the food, setting out plates, while the other four are lounging around, busy on their phones. One is a close relative of hers; I can tell by her scent. But she has none of my girl's spark, her vitality. The other three are kinda trashy. Like the groupies who used to hang around me back in the day, when I lived a totally different life. I can tell they're not Callie's friends. They're the kind of girls who'll receive her generosity with thanks, then gossip about her behind her back.

What is she doing with them? They're not fit to lick her boots. I'm gonna snatch her away. Treat her like the queen she is.

But how can I?

Reality comes crashing down.

I can't.

I used to take whatever I wanted. But not anymore.

Even though I've never wanted anything like I want Callie.

I did a deal with the devil, and this is my life now: the lonely existence of a solitary bear, who's never going to take a mate. It's no more than I deserve.

But there's no way I can stay away from Callie either.

She's the one chosen for me by fate—at least she would be, if I was allowed to make a choice.

I'll just have to follow her instead. Keep watch over her. And hope that will be enough for my beast.

"Ready," she calls. Her voice rings through my ears for the first time. The voice of an angel. If I could spend the rest of my life listening to it and nothing else, I'd be a lucky man.

She turns her head and looks for the others. I hold my breath as her gaze sweeps the clearing.

And comes to rest on me again.

My heart almost beats out of my chest.

She knows I'm here.

Because she's mine.

She blinks, and takes two wandering steps toward me again. She's behind the fire, and its glow illuminates her features. My girl is more beautiful than I could've imagined.

Desire pours through me like lava.

I'm a second away from doing something I'll regret.

3

Callie

I hear them before I even open my eyes. Gossiping like a swarm of buzzing bees. Plotting something. I listen hard. That name again—Jason Trentino. Wait—Lindsay is speaking, too. Which means she's no longer snoring beside me. I open my eyes. Her sleeping bag is indeed unoccupied. Weird. My big sister is not usually an early bird.

Also weird that I didn't notice her leaving. I had a hell of a night, tossing and turning, trying to get comfortable on the hard ground. Worrying about bear attacks. And, *wooh, those dreams.*

They flood back to me on a tide of heat. I was dreaming about some incredibly handsome man undressing me. Calling me beautiful. Touching me all over. He was naked, too. I've never seen a naked man before, but I wasn't embarrassed, I was incredibly aroused—

Umm, like I am right now. There's an ache between my thighs, and if I shuffle around a little, I'm pretty sure my panties are wet. Oh, god, did I, like, have a wet dream?

I swear I've never seen this guy in real life before, but the image of him is so vivid in my mind. A rugged, hyper-masculine face; all hard jaw and slicing cheekbones. Big brown eyes that soften the hard angles a little. The kind of longish, messy dark hair that you just want to run your hands through. And that body. One dreamy, rippling muscle after another. Incredible washboard abs. Thick, tree trunk-like thighs. And as for the firehose located between them—

"No, *I'll* go first—"

The voices are getting louder. They're bickering about something.

I try to tune them out. Maybe I'll slide my hand into my panties. I've never touched myself before, but right now I feel like a volcano that's gonna blow if I don't get some relief.

"—when we get to the cabin—"

The cabin?

I jerk bolt upright. When I got back from seeing it, I didn't mention it to the others, because I thought there was no point freaking them out. But it's been playing on my mind ever since. Part of me knows we should get the hell away from it. Whoever lives there is obviously hella keen to guard their privacy, and might be hostile to intruders.

But the other part of me is kinda curious. There was something real cozy about it. When I saw it, I thought *home*. For no reason at all.

But now, these airheads are talking about it, too? Something is definitely not right.

Okay, time to get up and find out what they're up to. I zip open my tent. The others are facing away from me, so I grab my washbag and water bottle and creep out. Crouching on the far side of the tent, I brush my teeth, wash my face, and try to tame my hair a little.

When I re-emerge, they're starting to walk out of the camp.

"Hey, girls," I call. "What's going on?"

Lindsay spins around fast. The other three curl their lips at me.

"Oh, hey, Callie. We're just gonna go make some TikTok videos," Lindsay says offhandedly.

"Cool, I'll come, too." I make my voice upbeat.

"Oh, it's nothing you'd be interested in, little sis." She steps over and ruffles my hair. Yes, she actually *ruffles my hair*, like I'm five years old.

"It'd be a big help if you could watch over our stuff though, hun." Brittany flashes me her whitened teeth and fake lips.

"Okay," I agree, shrugging my shoulders.

I stand and watch as they leave the clearing together.

Then I count to twenty and follow after them.

* * *

THEY'RE HEADING toward the river, of course.

To the cabin.

They're going slow, stumbling through the trees. Lindsay's having a lot of trouble navigating and it takes a long time. But at last, there's a shriek of excitement, which ends in a kind of muffled sound, as if someone clapped their hand over the shrieker's mouth.

"Ashley—!" I hear Lindsay hiss, and I break into a grin. It would be kinda funny if these airheads sabotaged their own scheme.

I take a few steps closer, then I duck behind a big old fir tree. I can see the cabin from here. My heart beats fast.

When Lindsay, Madison and Ashley climb the steps and stride right up to the front door, thumbs hooked into the straps of their silly backpacks, I almost choke on my own spit. Every bit of me wants to yell, *Get the hell away from there!* but somehow, I'm paralyzed. And where's Brittany?

Oh, she's filming on her phone. Of course, she is.

But who the hell is in there?

Looks like I'm just about to find out.

Lindsay knocks on the door. Softly at first, then harder.

I stop breathing.

There's no answer, for a long, long time.

No one's home.

I start breathing again. We're not going to get shot by some half-crazed mountain man.

Then Madison clears her throat. "Hellooo!" she trills.

I cringe as her loud, fake voice reverberates through the forest.

"We're looost! Can you please help us?" Ashley calls in a pathetic mewling tone.

Time ticks by, but there's only silence. Good. Maybe whoever lives here has gone on vacation to Aruba, or wherever mountain man go when they need a change of scene.

Guess the girls will be coming back now. I'd better go, so they don't see me. I start to step away, just as Lindsay grabs the handle of the front door and turns it.

"Oh, my god, it opens," she gasps.

"Go in!" one of the others squeaks. "Maybe we'll find some evidence or something."

Evidence?

We're all dead.

I watch in horror as all four girls creep through the door, one at a time. There's a ton of whispering, and... a wild roar. An earth-shattering sound that booms from the cabin.

What the heck was that? I swear every single one of my hairs stands on end. It sounded like a bear or something. Shit, did they just disturb a snoozing grizzly?

Suddenly, the air is full of high-pitched screams, and all four of them burst out of the cabin and sprint back the way they came, arms flailing, mouths hanging open. It'd be funny if I wasn't so darn freaked right now.

A moment later, a huge, dark shape fills the doorway. Holy crap. I make out thick, brown fur, dark, glistening eyes, and a set of gigantic white fangs... and, it's heading right at me!

I don't stop to think. I unclip the can of bear spray

from my utility belt, flick open the lid, and blast the giant grizzly right in the face.

I'm so fricking scared, I squeeze my eyes shut, but I keep going and going, releasing one blast after another.

Somewhere in my fog of terror, I hear the beast bellow. But it's a sound more of annoyance than pain.

And shit, the can is empty. I keep jabbing with my finger, but nothing happens.

"Jesus Christ, stop, already!" A deep voice roars.

Whuh? My eyes snap open.

There's no bear standing there.

Instead, there's a man.

A huge, muscular, buck-naked man.

Whose eyes are boring into me like hot coals.

What the hell?

He rubs at his eyes, which are kinda bloodshot. "What the fuck was that?" he bellows.

"B-bear spray."

"What?"

My hand trembles as I show him the can.

"Bear spray?" He snatches it and examines the label. Gosh, he's handsome. Like movie-star handsome. In fact, he looks a lot like the super-sexy guy in my dream last night—

He lets off a snarl of disgust and hurls the can on the ground. Then he fixes me with his searing gaze.

"You think this can of crap is going to scare off a grizzly who wants to claim you?"

"C-claim me?"

He shakes himself. "I mean, devour you." He takes a

step closer. "Swallow you whole. Like a little rabbit." His eyes are blazing. Dark and hot... and hungry.

I blink rapidly. "B-but the grizzly disappeared...?"

He snarls again. "Right."

"But, my friends..."

"Your friends are fine."

I frown. I'm so confused right now. All I know is that my body is responding to this incredibly hot, naked guy. And when I say responding, I mean my nipples are tingling and that little spot between my thighs is aching like crazy. Wow. I used to wonder if I was frigid, because I'd never felt turned on by another person before.

But nope. I just hadn't met the hottest guy on the planet before.

His stare is so intense, it's hard to maintain eye contact. But when I drop my gaze, I wind up staring at his cock.

It's huge. Not that I've seen one in real life before, but this one seems to be built on a different scale. It's beer-can thick, with veins running down it, and it hangs down between his thighs like a tree branch. But it's also, like semi-erect? I remember guys at school talking about having a semi.

Is that because he's looking at me?

No, that's ridiculous. He's so far out of my league, it's funny.

But I swear, the longer I stand there, the bigger his cock seems to get. Something crazy bursts into my mind—I imagine him snatching me up, carrying me into his cabin and busting through my virginity with that huge, thick rod. My cheeks and pussy burn in tandem.

"I-I'm sorry we disturbed you. I should go." I thumb over my shoulder.

He shakes his head. "You can't just leave like that."

My attention darts from his face to his cock and back again. "What do you mean? I need to go find my friends."

He curls his lip. "Tell me what you all were doing here."

I swallow hard. I could go with the story that we were lost. But I don't want to lie to him. He might be a crazy, naked psychopath for all I know, but for some reason, I feel like he's a good guy. Like I can trust him.

So, I explain that I thought we just hiking in the wilderness, but the others had some plan, involving TikTok or Instagram or something, which I wasn't privy to.

Anger tightens his jaw, then he narrows his eyes. "You didn't know what they were up to?"

I shake my head. "I know they've been cooking something up, but that's all. My sister and I are not real close, to be honest. And I'm not friends with the others. I'm only here because it's my sister's bachelorette weekend—"

I stop short, because something new is flooding those beautiful brown irises—relief?

"Go on," he says.

"I woke up this morning, and saw they were about to head off into the trees, so I decided to follow them. Then I saw…" I break off, overcome by shame. "One of them filming, while the other three knocked on your door, then let themselves in."

He works his jaw back and forth. "You know why they were doing this?"

"No."

He keeps on staring at me with those mesmerizing eyes. A shiver goes through me. Right now I do feel like a rabbit, caught in a car's headlights. Or, caught in the gaze of some apex predator, more like.

"You don't know me, do you?" he demands.

I shake my head. "Well, you look a lot like a guy I dreamed about last night."

"You dreamed about me?"

Crap. I can't believe I just admitted that. "Uh huh," I mumble as my cheeks burn.

A slow smile spreads across his face, and he lets out what can only be described as a purr. A deep, growly, bear's purr.

He takes a step toward me. "What happened in the dream?"

Oh, god. Now my cheeks are on fire. "Oh, I-I can't remember."

"Tell me." He takes a second step. "It's important."

And now I'm staring at his cock again, which I swear is more erect than before.

"I-I've got to go," I yelp.

I turn on my heel, and *bolt.*

4

Jason

"Run, little rabbit," I mutter as my girl's pert, round ass disappears into the trees. "It won't be long before I catch you and claim you." My bear is straining to go after her, of course. Strip off her clothes and claim her right on the forest floor. But I rein it in.

I'm buck naked, I remind it. Humans aren't cool with that. They get freaked out at having conversations with guys who have their dicks out.

She kept glancing at my cock though. I hope it didn't scare her. Wasn't my fault that it got harder and harder the more she looked at it.

And now, it's hard as a rock. Automatically, I wrap my hand around it. Her nipples were hard, too, poking sweetly through the fabric of her hiking shirt. And she kept running the tip of her tongue across her lips.

She's attracted to me. Of course, she is, because she's my mate.

I've finally found her.

And she has no idea who I am. I saw the truth in those gorgeous hazel eyes of hers.

She really is perfect.

I used to dream of meeting a girl who liked me for myself, not because of who she thought I was.

And here she is. The mate I never thought existed.

So beautiful and natural, and kind-hearted. I didn't need to read between the lines to understand that she's only here out of kindness to her sister, and she has nothing in common with that bunch of attention-addicts.

I can't wait to find out all about her. All about her dreams and passions; who her real friends are.

And what a gorgeous, curvy body. Big, round tits; lovely round ass. She even makes hiking gear look sexy. Damn, I wish she'd told me what her dream was about before she bolted. I could tell from the way her cheeks burned that it was something sexy. I wanted so bad to seduce her right there and then.

My hand is jerking up and down my cock. She smells like a peach, the moment before you sink your teeth into it. So ripe for mating, but untouched and innocent. I imagine stripping her clothes off her, piece by piece, and revealing her creamy flesh for the first time. I'll take her virginity outside, I decide. Lay her on a soft blanket and spread those thick thighs of hers—

A rope of hot cum shoots out the end of my cock, and splatters against a nearby tree. I keep pumping my fist furiously, squeezing out every last drop. Wishing it was flooding her pussy instead.

Soon, very soon, I promise myself. Next time I ejaculate, it's gonna be deep inside her. And I'm gonna breed her, impregnate her. I can't wait to fill her sweet belly with my young.

But first, I need to put some clothes on and make myself look respectable before I go hunt down my girl—

Halfway to the cabin, I stop dead.

What about those four airheads, though? They're probably broadcasting my whereabouts all over the Internet right now. I should go after them. Snatch their phones. Scare the life out of them.

I grind my teeth.

Protecting Callie or safeguarding my privacy?

There's no contest.

I hit the cabin steps at a run.

Callie

MY HEAD IS BURSTING with thoughts as I hurry back to the campsite. Wild, ridiculous thoughts. I don't even know his name, but I feel like I miss him already. How crazy is that? He's so mysterious, but so familiar at the same time. I can't explain it. It's like my soul already knows him.

But why did he ask me if I knew him?

He didn't just mean from my dream, of course.

And why did the girls stage that whole scene?

That moment—my brain keeps playing it over and over—when I sprayed the bear, then opened my eyes and *he* was there instead. And he didn't seem surprised that the bear had disappeared. It doesn't make any sense.

Crap. It's not easy running through dense wilderness at full pelt. Creepers keep catching at my ankles, and every few feet, another fallen branch trips me.

But there it is at last—I burst into the clearing... and stop dead.

The girls are not here. I was expecting to see them gathering up their things, but they're nowhere to be seen. The tent is still here, though, and so is Lindsay's backpack, and a bunch of other stuff. Doesn't look like they've been back.

Shit. They were scared senseless when they ran from the bear. They must've totally panicked, and probably headed off in the wrong direction.

I pull out my phone and call Lindsay.

There's no reception, of course.

This is not good, at all.

She has the map downloaded on her phone though. They'll be okay. I'm sure they're just focusing on getting out of the wilderness A-sap.

What about their stuff though? I survey the two tents and Lindsay's backpack. There's no way I can carry everything by myself. I could just wait, see if they come back.

But if I do that, I'll wind up having to spend another night out here.

Or... I could just go back to the cabin and ask the ridiculously sexy naked guy to help me out.

My clit gives a little jump.

No, not appropriate, Callie.

I pace around in a circle, trying to clear my thoughts.

If the girls aren't here now, they're not coming back. That much is obvious. I don't have a lot of food left, because I wound up giving most of it to the others last night. I'm vulnerable here, alone and without my bear spray.

I'm just gonna go. That's all I can do.

I pack up my sleeping bag and dismantle my tent, and shove everything into my backpack.

Wow, these straps do not feel good on my shoulders. My skin feels rubbed raw.

Guess that'll push me to walk faster though.

I cast one final look the girls' abandoned stuff, and I head off, in the direction we came from yesterday.

I've been walking for about ten minutes when I spot something pink, lying right in the middle of the trail. I hurry over to it, my back protesting under the weight of my pack.

It's Brittany's silly pink backpack. I pick it up and examine it. It's not damaged; there's no sign that it's been mauled by a bear. Does this mean they are nearby? I lift my head and yell each of their names into the trees.

But the only reply is the rustling of wind in the branches.

A shiver runs down my back.

Why would Brittany have taken off her backpack? Did something scare them, and they ran off in a panic? A cold feeling goes through me. Are they even together?

How the hell am I going to find them?

Go back to the cabin, a voice in my head says. *Sexy naked man will help you.*

I close my eyes for a moment, let the thought filter through me. It feels warm, comforting. My heart feels light and open. He's a good guy. He didn't mean me any harm.

I feel like my soul is speaking now.

But that's crazy.

How can I know this about him? He was hanging around naked, like that was normal. And he seems to share his cabin with a grizzly bear. He might be all kinds of deranged and dangerous.

I've got to keep going, retracing our path from yesterday. That's the only sensible thing I can do.

I readjust my backpack on my shoulders and keep plunging along the trail, praying I find the girls before nightfall.

5

Jason

I follow Callie along the trail at a distance, making sure to stay just out of view. It's not easy, because she keeps turning around and peering intently into the trees. She looks so vulnerable out here, all alone and unprotected. My heart aches. I yearn to run to her, take her in my arms and soothe away her sufferings.

Show every damn bear in this wilderness that she's mine.

Because I'm not the only shifter here, that's for sure. And as soon as they get a whiff of her intoxicating scent, it'll be all-out war here. I can't wait until she bears my mark on her neck, proving to the whole world that she's my property.

I watch as Callie picks up the backpack belonging to

one of those trashy girls. When she throws it down in despair, my chest hurts. And when lifts her head and yells their names into the sky, each pained cry is like a knife wound in my gut. I can't stand to see her hurting. Her pain is my own. And that's how it's going to be forever, because she's my mate—the other half of my soul.

I'm torn, and that's not an easy sensation for my beast to deal with. It's bellowing and straining inside me.

Those damn friends of hers. I grit my teeth. If it wasn't for them, I'd seduce her, take her back to my cabin right now, and show her what it means to be a bear's mate. But they've gone and gotten themselves lost, and I know she won't leave until she finds them.

I shouldn't let them see me again. If they didn't manage to video me earlier, they will now. The best thing I can do is follow her, keep watch over her until she finds the others and guides them out of the wilderness.

Trouble is, their scents are coming from all directions. They scattered when they ran from my cabin, and my nose is telling me they haven't managed to find each other yet.

At least Callie is on the right track. The scent in front of her is strong and true. If she keeps going, she'll find at least one of the girls.

And then what? They'll leave the forest together, and how will I find her again?

Now! my bear roars. *Take her, she's yours.*

Before I can stop myself, I call, "Hey, there! Wait up!"

Callie gives a little gasp of shock and spins to face me. Her face is frozen with fear, and it's yet another knife in the gut. Her hand goes to her waist, then she fumbles around for something. Bear spray. My beast surges inside me. The blast she gave me earlier is still stinging its nostrils.

I crook an eyebrow. "You aren't gonna spray me again, are you?"

"How did you find me?" she demands, her voice high and tight.

My insides crumple. She doesn't trust me, yet. She thinks I'm a stalker. I can't blame her.

"I followed your scent," I tell her, because she's whip-smart and I know that's the only thing that'll convince her.

She wrinkles her nose. "What do you mean?"

I take a long breath and release it slowly. I'm thirty-four years old and I've managed to get through my life without ever having to explain my nature to a human.

Okay, here goes.

"Earlier, when you sprayed the grizzly, it didn't go anywhere, did it?"

Her lovely arched eyebrows tug together. "I-I guess it ran away fast."

"You know that's not true."

Her frown gets deeper, then she bites her lip. It's an incredible sight, her plump lower lip disappearing between her pearl white teeth, and my cock starts to ache again.

"It kind of—disappeared—and then you were there, right in its place."

"But that's not possible, right?"

She nods uncertainly, eyes shining with intelligence.

"That's because me and the bear are the same. I'm a shapeshifter."

"Shapeshifter?" she mouths.

"Give me your hand."

When I step toward her, I half expect her to freak out, but instead, she lays her small, soft hand in my massive one. My heart soars. The very first contact between us. Soon, she'll be in my arms, her sweet curvy body entwined with mine, all naked. Soon, her soft thighs will be wrapped around my waist, while her virgin pussy grips my cock.

But first I need to introduce her to my bear. Show her she can trust me. Gently, I raise her hand and press it again my big, beary chest, right at the spot when my heartbeat is strongest.

She blinks. "Wow, that's strong," she murmurs.

"Now, feel this." I move her hand to the center.

"What's that?... it's like a kind of rumble." When her eyes meet mine, they're flooded with green forest light. She looks like a beautiful woodland sprite.

"It's how my breath sounds. Because I'm half-man and half-bear."

"You change into one, and then the other?"

"Yup."

"That's why you were naked?"

"Uh huh—" I break off. Because she has *that* look in her eyes again. That flash of naked lust. Desire pours through me. It's getting harder to control myself by the second.

"Shifters are naked a lot of the time," I tell her. It's probably too early to share that with her, but what the hell. She's gonna have to get used to it.

She scans my white T-shirt and jeans.

"I put these on for you," I say. "So I didn't scare you."

"I wasn't scared before. I mean, not real scared." She looks a little surprised by her own words, like she's not fully in control of them. My chest warms. She's letting her instincts take the lead. I feel her opening to me, her soul and mine reaching out for each other.

"That's because you were drawn to me. You could feel it, couldn't you?"

"Yes," she says softly.

Her hand hasn't left my chest. Now, she slides it up until it curves around the back of my neck. It's cool and delicious and as arousing as hell.

Like I'm in a dream, I dip my head and crush my mouth against hers.

Soft, so soft. She lets out a little moan and right away, she opens for me. I plunge my tongue in and claim her sweet mouth. I feel her own little tongue dancing against it, while her hand grips my neck tighter. I wrap my arms around her, draw her in close. I feel the pebbles of her nipples pressing against my chest. Shit, she's really aroused. My sexy, sexy girl. I sneak my hand up the back of her shirt and reach for her bra clasp. In a second it's undone, and I feel the weight of her breasts as they're released from their constraints.

I want to be gentle with her, savor every moment,

but my beast is taking over, and before I know it, I'm yanking her shirt up, desperate to see them.

They're even more beautiful than I imagined, big and creamy, with rose-colored nipples. I clasp them in my rough hands, kneading at them. Then I drop to my knees in the dirt and worship them with my tongue. When I suck one of her little buds into my mouth, she gives a cry. She's sensitive. I suck on one, then the other, and she pulls my hair and presses her little pussy against me, desperate to grind it. A grin spreads across my face. She's so ripe, so ready. I knew from the way she kept looking at my cock earlier that she was a passionate one.

Of course, she is; she's gonna have to get used to me fucking her every day from now on. Multiple times a day.

I slide my hand up and cup her crotch through her hiking pants. When I feel how hot and damp she is, my cock surges again. She lets out another moan.

You like that?" I growl.

"Mhmm," she mutters.

I put my free hand around the back of her neck and draw her down, make her kiss me, while I press my fingers against her slit.

"Show me," I growl.

I don't have to tell her twice. She starts grinding her little pussy against my fingers.

"Go on," I whisper, and she mewls and pants into my mouth.

"Time we pulled these off," I say. I hook my fingers into

the waistband of her pants and tug them down, along with her panties. She gives a squeak of surprise as I shove them down to her ankles. Her bra and shirt are bunched up under her arms, and in between, her lovely body is completely bare, exposed to my gaze. As I glimpse her pussy for the very first time, I almost blow my load. Beneath a neat, dark strip, it's perfectly pink and glistening with her arousal. I back her up against a nearby tree trunk and push her ankles further apart to get a better look.

I feel like I'm dreaming. My beautiful mate, naked and vulnerable, trusting me enough to get her in this position where she couldn't run away, even if she wanted to.

As if she just read my mind, a flicker of uncertainty passes across her eyes. "My friends—" she mutters.

"Are nowhere near. But later I'll shift into my bear and I'll be able to track them down in minutes. Don't worry about them; they're safe. And there's no one else —whether human or shifter—around for miles."

I kneel back and gaze at her while she absorbs that information. I love that she doesn't try to hide her body from me. She just stands there and lets me look.

When her tongue darts out and licks her lips, my cock jolts. She wants this. She trusts me. Good. Soon she'll learn that I only ever have her best interests at heart.

"I want to see you again," she says in a quiet voice.

My breath catches in my throat. "My body, you mean?"

"Uh huh." Her eyes are dark now, almost black.

Because her pupils are dilated with desire, I realize. This girl is incredible.

"You liked seeing me naked?" I go to pull up my shirt.

She nods eagerly, her gaze lasering in on my crotch. I'm not surprised. My dick is jutting out like a flagpole beneath my jeans. It's so hard it hurts, and it's taking all my self-control not to release it from its prison.

"First, I need to teach you a lesson," I say.

Her mouth forms a little O of surprise. "What for?" she says innocently.

"For blasting me in the face with a whole can of bear spray."

Her cheeks turn pink. "I'm sorry about that, but I thought you were going to eat me. I was just protecting myself—"

"I am going to eat you," I cut in, staring at her drenched little pussy. "Right after I've spanked you."

"Spanked me?" she breathes.

"I'm going to spank you." I straighten up one leg, turning my thigh into a perfect spanking bench. "Over my knee."

She bites her lip, but there's no hiding the tell-tale flush heating her cheeks and the brightness of her eyes.

"You think you deserve it?" I say.

She hesitates, then nods.

"Then show me."

Her eyes get even brighter, then she shuffles over to me, pants and panties hobbling her steps. I take her hand to steady her. She's a virgin, totally untouched, but she's acting purely on instinct. She kneels between my legs, then she bends her body over my left thigh. I wait, hands quivering, but not touching her until her creamy ass is raised up. Holy hell. What an incredible sight. Two round pale globes, right over my knee. When I lay my hand on her at last, she quivers at my touch. Her skin is even more velvety than I expected. At first I just stroke her, one cheek, then the other, gradually easing her thighs wider apart. She sighs and relaxes under my touch, revealing her pink pussy to my gaze. I can see her tiny virgin entrance and the rosebud of her asshole, glistening with her arousal.

"I'm going to spank you six times, one for each blast of bear spray you gave me."

"Okay," she murmurs.

I keep my hand real light, just enough pressure to raise a pretty pink blush to her skin.

"One," she mutters when I bring my hand down on her right cheek.

I close my eyes, savoring the word. She's a natural. I alternate sides, and with every slap she sighs then gasps out the number. Two—three—four—five—six spanks of my hand, raining down on her lovely ass.

Too soon, I'm done and the intoxicating scent of her arousal rises to my nostrils, stronger than ever. I pause for a moment, admiring my handiwork, then I stroke her warm flesh with my fingertips, easing the punishment away.

"Did you like that?" I ask.

"Yes," she moans.

I slide my hand down and touch her bare pussy for the first time. She jolts under my touch. So goddamn sensitive. It's beautiful. The tip of my finger naturally slides into her entrance. But only half an inch, and it won't go any further.

Shit. My cock is gonna need to force its way through her maidenhead. I can hardly wait.

But first I need to taste her.

I stand her up again and bury my face between her thighs. She tastes like the sweetest cherry blossom nectar. I dive in deep, lapping up all the juices from her wet, swollen pussy, while she moans and sighs.

It's not long before her legs begin to quake.

"Jason, I can't…!" she wails.

Stifling a grin, I grip her sweet ass in both hands, supporting her until the quake turns into an almighty explosion. She throws her head back and screams up at the sky while she comes on my tongue. It's fucking beautiful. My wild goddess. The perfect mate for a big, growly bear like me.

"Oh, gosh." She giggles, pressing the back of her hand to her lips. "I didn't know I'd be like that."

"Like what?" I ask innocently

"You know… loud." Her cheeks flush.

"Be as loud as you like, honey. That's a big part of why I live here—" I break off as a thought occurs to me. "How did you know my name?"

"Oh, the girls kept whispering about some Jason Trentino."

I gaze deep into her hazel eyes. They're as limpid and earnest as ever. She has no idea who Jason Trentino is. "And you figured, that's who they were looking for. Who did you think he was?"

She shrugs. "Some celebrity. Since that's pretty much all they care about. That and modifying their appearances until I literally can't tell the difference between Brittany and an inflatable sex doll."

I laugh. "Sounds like you're not into all that."

She blows out a puff of air. "I only watch old movies, really. But, mostly I like to read."

I close my eyes for a beat, savoring her. I'd started to think there was no one in the world who hadn't seen my shameful video and fall from grace.

But here she is; this beautiful, pure spirit, not corrupted by this superficial, attention-hungry era.

"You're a big deal, aren't you?" she bursts out.

I take her hand. "I'm not going to tell you right now. I want you to get to know me first. See if you like me, as I am."

Her pretty lips curve into a smile. "I like you," she says sweetly.

I stop breathing. This angel likes me. That's more than I could've asked for.

Then she frowns. "Didn't you promise to get naked again?"

I grin. I did.

Now, my beast urges. *Claim her. She's ready.* She is. Her ripe, fertile scent is the only thing I can smell right now. Her pussy is so wet it's unreal, and my dick is throbbing, demanding release. I could be inside her in a minute, her sweet pussy clenching around me.

She deserves better than this, though. My cock is the only one that's ever going to be inside her. I'm not gonna rush this. I want her first time to be special. Want to take my time with her. Give her my mark at the same time.

"Hold that thought," I say. "We'd better find your friends first."

She sighs. "Guess you're right."

6

Callie

I don't want to know who Jason Trentino is. Because, when I find out, it'll all be over. He'll go back to his glittering celebrity life, and I'll be nursing my poor aching heart, and the memory of him stripping me and making me orgasm in the middle of the forest.

I want to hang onto this time with him for as long as possible. I feel like we're in some kind of suspended reality here, where a famous guy, who's also half grizzly bear, is interested in a dumpy, plain nobody.

But I'm also burning with questions. What is he doing living in a cabin, deep in the wilderness, like a crazy mountain man? Why was my sister so eager to find him that she even turned this trip into her bachelorette party?

I keep shoving them down as I follow him through the forest trail. As soon as we started walking, he took my hand, and he hasn't let it go. I love the feeling of his huge, rough hand enveloping my own. Tingles won't quit running through me. He's walking at a steady pace, not fast, and I'm so glad for that. I'm in no hurry to get to our destination.

We've got a plan—we're going to hunt the four of them down and observe them. Hopefully Lindsay will be leading them all to the exit, and they won't even know we're there. They won't get to lay eyes on him again.

And then?

I keep thinking, what if that was my one chance to have sex with him? What if he just leads me to the trailhead and says, thanks for the memories?

It'll be enough, I tell myself.

But that's not true. The thought of him disappearing from my life just about cuts me in two.

Jason says he's picked up their trail, but it's weirdly faint. They're not on the main trail, but most likely took a 'shortcut'.

"And that's how most tourists fail to make it out of here," he says grimly.

I gasp. "Are their lives in danger?"

He turns his head toward me. I lock onto his searing gaze, and again, I'm rewarded with a lurch in my chest. That unearthly sign that tells me we're connected.

"Not at all. I promise you, Callie, hand on heart, I will find them and make sure they get out of here. Even the one who was filming me."

"Oh, you can leave her behind," I say with a snicker.

"Hopefully they've learned an important lesson today."

I roll my eyes. "Don't bank on it. None of them are famous for their attention spans."

He huffs out a dry laugh. "You and your sister are real different, huh?"

"You can say that again."

"You don't even look alike."

My head snaps toward him again. "You know which one of them is my sister?"

"Of course. She smells different from you, but I could tell you're related."

I bite my lip. I've got a lot to learn about this bear thing.

"Can you, like smell me all the time?" I hardly dare ask, but I have to know.

"Yup." He nods thoughtfully. "When I first picked up your scent yesterday, it was the most incredible thing I'd smelled in my life."

I go still. "Yesterday?"

"Yeah, when you stumbled over to my cabin."

My mouth falls open. "You saw me then?"

"I arrived too late to see you, but I followed you back. I couldn't help myself." A sexy smile tugs at the corners of his lips. "I knew which one you were right away. You're so different from the others."

Well, that's nothing new. I've always felt like an ugly duckling around my sister and her friends. The chubby one. The butt of their jokes.

"So much more beautiful. You just had this glow

about you," he continues. "I saw how hard you were working, while they were busy with their phones. And when you turned and looked in my direction, I just knew—"

I give a little gasp. "I remember! Something made me look into the trees. It was nothing I saw or heard. It was more like something spoke, deep inside me..."

"The voice of your mate," he says.

"Mate?" I whisper.

He nods. "We shifters take mates. We don't date. We stay single until we find our mate. The one we're supposed to be with..." He looks so serious, tingles race through me and my heart pounds like crazy.

"And then?"

"And then we claim her. Show the whole world she's our property."

"How?" I whisper.

"With our cocks, and our teeth," he growls.

My mouth falls open. Becoming Jason's property is the most exciting thing I can imagine—

He stops dead, and takes a deep sniff.

"What is it?"

"They're close by. Or at least, some of them are."

"This way." He leads me off the trail and directly into the trees.

I shake myself, trying to focus on the task at hand. But it's not easy when I *think* Jason just implied that I might be his mate?

He keeps his tread light and I follow his lead. I kinda like this stalking thing. The forest seems to be getting darker and the trees are crowding closer together, and suddenly, the ground ahead of us disappears. There's a sheer drop. Jason pushes me behind him and advances closer to the edge.

"They're here," he says in a low voice. "Or at least, your sister and one of the others. But I think someone's hurt."

"No!" I dart forward. Despite everything, I can't stand the thought of Lindsay suffering.

Jason steadies me while I peer over the edge of a precipice.

Lindsay and Ashley are down there, on the forest floor, and there's a terrible keening sound coming from them. My stomach clenches.

Lindsay's face is covered in dirt, and possibly some cuts as well, while Ashley's leg is bent at an unnatural angle.

"Oh, my god!" I clap my hand over my mouth.

"Looks like it's broken," Jason whispers in my ear. "Ashley is freaking out, and your sister is asking her to calm down so she can think." He pauses, listening. Lindsay grabs onto a big rock and levers herself upright, but when she puts her weight on her right leg, she cries out in pain and crumples to the ground again.

"She's saying, it hurts like hell," Jason whispers. "There's no way I can walk on it. What the fuck are we going to do?"

I watch them pick up their phones, examine the screens, then drop them again.

"There's no reception," I mutter. I look at my own phone, try to dial, but nothing happens.

"The coverage is real spotty out here," Jason says. His

voice is tense. I glance at him. His jaw is set and his fists are clenched. I can practically feel the energy radiating off him. "Hell," he mutters, working his jaw back and forth. "I'm going down there."

I let out a gasp. "Jason, no, you can't! You can't let them see you again."

He shakes his head. "Trust me, it's the last thing I want to do. But they need help."

Shivers run through me. After everything they've done, he's still willing to help them. My man has a massive heart. My own heart fills with warmth. With love. Yes, I'm falling for this incredible guy. Everything is happening so fast, but it all feels so right.

"Can you take me to the trailhead? Or wherever I can get phone coverage?" I say. "I'll call mountain rescue."

Jason's expression is grim. "That'll take a couple of hours. Then it'll take the rescue service a long while to arrive. There's nowhere for a helicopter to land out here."

I see emotions working behind his eyes as he turns his thoughts over. His body is pressing against mine, muscles all bunched up. He feels like a tightly-coiled spring.

I understand enough to know that letting the girls see him again will destroy him, and I can't stand the thought of that.

"There's no way I can let you do this," I blurt out.

The look he gives me is so full of admiration and warmth, I swoon a little bit.

Then his face hardens. "I need to get them out of here," he says.

My stomach drops like an elevator.

7

Callie

$\mathcal{I}$ plant my hands on my hips. "Jason Trentino, I have no idea who you are to the rest of the world, and I don't care. All I know is you're an incredible human being—uh, shifter—and if you want to live alone in the wilderness, that's your business. My sister has already tried to ruin that for you. If you go help them now, you'll be all over TikTok tomorrow."

He shrugs. "I'm pretty sure the damage has been done already."

"I wouldn't bank on it. If I know them, they'll spend a few days working on the videos, applying a bunch of filters before they launch them on social media. Especially something this big."

A smile tugs at the corners of his lips. "You think I'm big, huh?"

"Yup." Before I can stop myself, my attention is flickering down to his crotch again.

"I'll show you just how big later," he growls, following my gaze.

Damn. Who knew it was possible to get aroused in such a tense situation?

"I'll go grab their phones," I say as an idea finally emerges from my shocked brain. "In exchange for your help. Make them promise not to say a word."

This time, a soft smile crosses Jason's lips. He takes my hand and kisses it. "You're a sweetheart, Callie. But I know people like this, believe me. They can't help themselves."

I bite down on the end of my tongue, because he's right. Attention is like oxygen for Ashley, Brittany and Madison. Without it, I think they'd just cease to exist. Shrivel up and die.

"If I hadn't found you, I wouldn't be here now, and that matters to me more than a thousand online exposés, believe me."

My heart pounds as those chocolate brown eyes gaze into mine, soft with devotion. He's doing all this *for me*. Giving up his privacy, his mountain man lifestyle… I feel so special, so loved. I blink fast before I start to tear up.

"You're going to shift, right?" I say slowly, as another idea occurs to me.

He nods seriously. "Yeah, I need to carry them out of here. I'll be able to carry all three of you, no sweat. But I'm wondering about the other two."

"Maybe they're on their way out of the forest

already?"

He shakes his head "I don't think so. I picked up their scents a while back, heading in exactly the wrong direction. And they're not even together. It'll be dark in a few hours. I don't like the idea of them being in the forest alone. They'll be prey to a bunch of shifters, *and* non-shifters."

I shiver, understanding he means full-blooded grizzlies.

"I can go find them—?"

"No!" He cuts me off. "There's no way I'm leaving you alone here, Callie. You're under my protection; now and forever."

I stare at him in a shocked silence. Did he just say *forever*?

"Argh!" A loud wail comes from the bottom of the cliff. I peer over again. Ashley is fretting. Even from here, I can see the angry purple color of her ankle.

"I'm calling in some reinforcements," Jason announces.

I frown. "How?"

He flashes his sexy grin. "As bears do." He tears his T-shirt over his head, and I understand.

"Wait—the girls don't need to see you as a human, do they?"

A light comes into his eyes. "Not if someone else can do the talking."

I jab a thumb at my chest. "That'll be me. Don't worry, I've got it under control."

He doesn't ask me anything else. Instead, he gives me a look full of trust.

Then he strips his jeans off, and I watch as the most incredible thing I've ever seen happens. The bones in his face broaden, his shoulders get a lot wider and hunch forward, fur sprouts all over him. There's a bunch of cracks and snaps, and suddenly, a huge grizzly bear is standing in front of me, on all fours. I could be terrified, but I'm not, because he still has Jason's beautiful, soulful eyes. And he's my mate.

This time, I can't hold back my tears. There's something so special, so intense about seeing him in his bear form. Impulsively, I hold out my arms and run to him. I wrap them around his massive, massive neck, and bury my face in his fur. And, wow, it's soft. I thought it would be rough, but it's actually incredibly luxurious, and it has his familiar, spicy scent.

I hear him inhale deeply, drawing air into his massive lungs, then he lets out a long, ragged sigh. I draw back, sinking my hands into the soft fur of his cheeks, and press my lips to his nose. I'm acting purely on instinct, but it feels right. His nose feels like the softest leather, and my lips tingle at the contact. When I pull away from him at last, there's no mistaking the emotion in his eyes.

Thank you.

The word appears in my chest, right where my heart is. Because he said it. It didn't come from my brain, but from him. I have no idea how I know that; I just do.

I connected with his bear.

And now my love for him burns even stronger in my heart.

He backs up several steps, then he lifts his majestic head to the sky and *roars*.

It's an awesome sound. The forest shakes with it. Birds burst out of the trees and take flight. It goes on and on.

When it stops, my ears are ringing. He looks at me, lowers his body to the ground, and indicates over his shoulder.

He doesn't need to tell me twice. I know exactly what to do.

I run over and clamber onto his back. It's broad, but my legs instinctively cling to him like I've done this a hundred times before. I feel perfectly safe. I sink my fingers into the fur around his neck, steadying myself, and we're off.

And when I say *off*, I mean, we're going headfirst down the precipice.

Jason jumps from rock to rock. But his footing is sure and I sense that he's going more cautiously than he otherwise would. I just cling on tight and clench my teeth together to stop myself from screaming.

Sooner than I would've expected, we're on solid ground again, and the air is full of screams—not mine.

"Callie! Oh my god!" Lindsay wails. To her credit, she pulls herself to her feet, grabs a branch and waves it threateningly in Jason's direction. I'm a little bit proud of her.

As soon as Jason lowers his powerful body to the ground, I leap off and run to them.

"It's okay," I say. "He's not hurting me. I just made

friends with a big, kindly grizzly. Now, I need you to listen to me."

While Lindsay and Ashley's eyes get bigger and bigger, I explain exactly what needs to happen.

When I'm done, Lindsay holds out her phone with a trembling hand.

"Take it. We haven't uploaded anything," she says, her voice shaking. "I swear."

"And the other two?"

"I don't know. I haven't seen them since, since…" She bursts into tears.

I glance at Jason, and the pride shining in his eyes gives me strength. "We'll find them, don't worry. But we need to leave now—"

A long, throaty purring sound cuts off the end of my sentence. I spin around, look up, and I'm greeted by the sight of two huge grizzlies, staring down at us from the edge of the precipice. My hairs stand on end. But Jason lifts his head and makes a similar sound.

It's okay. They're just calling to each other. They're his buddies.

A moment later, they're bounding down the steep rockface, and here they all are, grappling each other in rough bear hugs. It's a scary sight, but I get it—they're communicating.

At last, they draw apart and one of them ambles over to Lindsay and the other goes over to Ashley.

Ashley gives a little scream, but I shush her.

"They're here to help you, so please don't try their patience," I tell her sternly.

She gapes at me. She's not used to me being assertive. She's more accustomed to me dropping my head and letting her insults and criticisms wash over me.

"Okay," she says meekly. I go over and help her stand up. Her leg looks pretty badly injured. The bear crouches down low and with my guidance, she throws her weight over its massive back.

By the time we're good to go, Lindsay has already climbed on the back of her furry steed. Right away, both bears head off, turning out of the small clearing like they know exactly where they're going.

I clamber onto Jason's back again. A sigh pours out of me. Sinking into his soft fur feels like coming home. I sure hope I'll get to spend a lot of time with his bear in future.

I expect him to follow the others, but instead, he turns the other way.

"Callie!" Lindsay wails. "Where are you going?"

"You'll be fine," I call to her. "When you get phone coverage, call the emergency services, and these guys will do the rest."

I wrap my arms more tightly around Jason's neck as he heads into the pine trees. I hear his big nostrils snuffling at the forest floor as he tries to locate Madison and Brittany's scent. He goes faster and faster. I cling on for dear life as he starts to run, darting in between the trees at breathtaking speed. He's so agile for a huge bear, never bumping into anything, keeping me safe.

The light is getting low when I spot a pair of pink daisy dukes, barely covering a skinny ass. Brittany. Thank goodness.

Jason ambles up beside her.

"I don't have time to explain," I yell above her panicked screaming. "Give me your phone and climb on behind me."

FIFTEEN MINUTES LATER, we find Madison. She's sitting on a tree stump, crying. She's broken a couple of her horrible purple talons, and her make-up has slid down her face, making her look strangely like a jack-o'-lantern, but she's otherwise unhurt.

I persuade her to clamber up, too, and now Jason is carrying all three of us. I'm on the front, of course. No way am I letting either of them get near my man.

The sun has set by now, and Jason picks his way through the forest more carefully as darkness pushes out the last of the twilight. It feels like a long time before we arrive at the trailhead. Or maybe it's just that I'm real impatient to have Jason to myself.

Brittany and Madison slide off his back, falling into an ungainly heap.

"You'll be okay now," I tell them.

"Aren't you staying with us?" Madison demands, a high note of panic in her voice.

"No, I'm staying here." I shrug. We've gotten them to safety. I don't owe them any more explanation.

Jason makes a long purring sound. I think I'm starting to speak bear already. It means, *let's go home.* Longing and excitement pour through me like liquid fire.

After a couple of minutes of walking, Jason stops. Beneath me, I feel something happening. Bones shifting and rearranging. Instinctively, I jump off his back, and a second later, the bear disappears, and here he is again— the gorgeous naked man I met this morning, who I feel like I've known forever.

His handsome features are drawn with concern as he looks me over. "How are you doing, baby?"

With a cry, I throw myself into his arms and press my head against his big, warm chest.

"It's okay, honey," he murmurs in my ear. "It's over now. They're all safe."

"Thank you, so, so much," I say. "I just hope they keep their word."

"Callie, listen to me." He holds me at arms' length. "I don't give a damn about their word. All I care about is you. And right now, I'm taking you home."

Home. The word, spoken in his sexy, growly voice vibrates through my ears like the sweetest song.

"Let's go," I say.

8

Jason

My mate is on my back. Her thighs are wrapped tight around my body, and her sweet face is nestled into my fur. I'm taking her home, and I'm gonna claim her at last. My blood is running in my veins like lava. All I can think about is plunging my cock into her tiny virgin pussy, and giving her the mark that will show every male in the world that she's mine. I could barely tolerate my buddies looking at her with lust in their eyes. Even though they were doing me a solid, my beast was ready to rip their heads off.

Well, I can't blame them. Anyone with a pulse would go crazy for her gorgeous curves.

But no one else is going to touch her. Ever.

My beast is charging faster, faster, desperate to get

her indoors. My night vision is flawless, and I could easily sprint flat out through the densest forests, but I hold it back, try to make the journey as comfortable as possible for my girl. She's been through so much today. It must be overwhelming. I hear her little sighs and gasps as my speed startles her, but I know she trusts me. I sense it deep in my soul.

The scent of my little cabin fills my nostrils yards before it appears. For years, it's been my hiding place. A barrier between me and the world. But now it's truly a home. Because I'm going to bring my mate here. I just hope that it'll be good enough for her.

She makes a little sound as the stout front door comes into view—kind of relief and anticipation mixed together. When I stop on the pathway, she slides off my back.

I don't waste any time. I force my beast back inside me and become a man again.

A naked man.

No point trying to hunt down a fig leaf now. The first time she saw me I was naked, and she didn't run away from my monster dick. I've even gotten the impression she kinda likes it.

Well, there'll be time for that soon.

But first, I'm gonna treat her like the princess she is.

I sweep her up in my arms, kick the front door open, and carry her over the threshold.

The soft, interior lights come on automatically, and she gives a little sigh of appreciation.

She likes it.

My beast bounds beneath my chest. I admit, it's a

pretty cozy cabin for a mountain man. First of all, it's a lot bigger than a typical mountain cabin. The front room is compact, but then the building extends way back. I need my space, even when I'm just storming around by myself.

Secondly, it's furnished in a style they call rustic chic. Being the always-in-the-public-glare guy I used to be, I didn't have access to genuine old furniture. Instead, I ordered it from some dumb, expensive-as-shit Hollywood store. But from Callie's reaction, I'm real glad I got it. I want her to be delighted by everything she sees, and so comfortable here she never even thinks of leaving.

She insists on taking off her shoes by the door, then she steps on my fur rugs with her beautiful bare feet, wriggling her toes delightedly.

I give her the grand tour, my excitement growing with every step.

She's adorable. She exclaims about this and that—the fitted kitchen with plenty of cooking stuff, the huge bathroom, with the hot tub in the corner and the extra-large rainforest shower. The three guest bedrooms; the study. As we approach the master bedroom, I can barely keep ahold of myself. My bear presses up against my skin as I open the door and I wind up slamming it back against its hinges. A little more dramatic than I intended.

She lets out a little gasp. Well, the bed is massive. Plenty of space for a big ol' grizzly and his mate to roll around all night. It's wooden, and so is all the furniture. The lighting is soft and the comforter is blue plaid, and for some reason, I changed the sheets this morning and piled a bunch of cushions over the pillows. Almost like I was expecting someone.

I watch as her gaze sweeps over the bed. Then it comes back to rest on me. On my face, my cock. Which is already sticking out at half-mast.

Damn.

She bites her lip, and I see a flash of nerves in her eyes. She wants it, but she's scared of it. That's so darn sexy. I bite back a roar of hunger, plant my hands on my hips and I let her look.

"Like what you see?" I growl.

"Uh huh," she says, her voice high and tight.

"This cock is gonna make you feel real good," I tell her. "I won't quit till you've come all over it."

She gives a little gasp, and her pretty eyes get bigger and bigger.

"I'm gonna bury it deep inside your little pussy, and fuck a dozen orgasms out of you."

Her cheeks flush and I hear her breath coming heavy and fast. See her big, round tits rising and falling.

"You like that?" I demand.

"Yes," she says, her little pink tongue darting out and moistening her lips.

"Then show me. Show me you're ready for me to take that little cherry of yours."

For a moment she holds real still, a pink blush creeping over her cheeks. Then she strips off her shirt, followed by her bra. Her beautiful, big tits tumble out again. So soft and creamy, with those tender little nipples, just begging to be sucked. Then, shyly, she slides her pants and panties down her thighs. The sweet scent of her arousal floods my nostrils. She's so ripe and ready for me. And my cock is so hard it hurts.

Blood roars in my veins as I drag her into my arms and kiss her senseless. I force her soft mouth open and plunge my tongue deep inside. At the same time, I cup her lovely tits, and squeeze her nipples.

She moans into my mouth. Then her soft hand closes around my throbbing shaft.

Fuck. I hiss out a groan.

"Like this?" she asks.

"Yeah, just like this, but you're gonna make me—"

I don't finish the sentence, because she's no longer standing in front of me. In a flash she's dropped down onto her knees and something even softer than her hand is closing around the end of my dick. I close my eyes, because if I even look at my mate sucking my dick, I'm gonna blow my load. I feel her tongue working over the head, and then her soft lips move right over the head as she takes more of me in. She slides back and forth, sucking on me, taking me in deeper each time. And the whole time, she sighs and groans like it's the sweetest thing she ever tasted. When I feel my dick hit the soft back of her throat, my eyes fly open automatically.

My beautiful girl, on her knees, taking my monster cock in her mouth, one hand between her thighs, working her clit, like sucking me is turning her on.

Fuck.

I start to move my hips, thrusting into her mouth. At first she chokes a little, then she adjusts herself, angles her head and lets me go in even deeper. Holy hell. What a woman.

My balls tighten. All I want is to shoot my load down her sweet virgin throat.

But no. The first time I come, it's gonna be inside her. I'm not gonna waste my seed. I'm gonna flood her with it, shoot it all the way up into her womb.

I pull out so fast, all she can do is stare up at me, her lips glistening and parted expectantly.

"Get on the bed," I tell her. She looks a little stunned, but she scrambles right up and walks over, her lovely round ass jiggling. There's the faintest pink marks left behind by my fingerprints. A fresh wave of desire pours through me again. I've got half a mind to turn her ass all nice and pink again, before I take her virginity.

Annnd… seems like she's got the same idea. Because she clambers up on her knees and leans over the pillows, giving me her lovely rear view.

I run my hand down the length of her back, and down to the soft, round globes of her ass.

"You want it like this?" I growl.

"Mhmm," she mutters. She's buried her face in the crook of her arms. When I slide my hand between her thighs and cup her pussy, she gives a wild cry.

She's even wetter than before. Her juices are running down her thighs. I press my fingertip against her hymen again, testing it. It's still right there, intact. My cock twitches as I imagine how it's gonna feel when I bust through it. I work her clit a little with a fingertip. "What do you want?"

"Your hand… on my ass," she gasps out.

Holy crap. My head rings. I'm dead. I raise my hand and give her left cheek a light tap.

"Like this?" I growl.

"Yeah."

"Want some more?"

"Yes…"

I love the way her voice is all breathy. And I get it—she likes it like this. Likes it wild and rough. Of course, she does. That's why she's the perfect mate for a bear. "Yes, what?"

"Yes, please."

Fuck.

I spank her again and again, swatting her ass until it's delectably pink all over. With each one, she releases a little cry of need.

While she's still panting for air, I take my cock in my other hand and press it to her entrance. She's dripping wet. Her little pussy draws me in, and suddenly I'm half an inch, then a whole inch.

"Ow," she cries out.

I pull out again. "It's okay, honey." I cover her shoulder with kisses. I'm being too rough, going too fast. I've gotta make this as special for her as it is for me.

I flip her onto her back and spread her thighs. What an incredible sight—her sweet pink pussy wet and spread open for me.

And it's just begging to be kissed. I dip my head and lick it all over, sighing at her honey-sweet virgin flavor. She gasps and groans and tugs at my hair. When her thighs start to tremble, I pull back and replace my tongue with my cock.

This time, it goes in a lot easier. I lean back and watch as it disappears between her sweet lips for the first time.

"Ahh!" she cries out, but at the same time, she reaches for me, wraps her arms around my back and pulls me to her. I feel my dick break through her hymen. Feel her tight little pussy pulsing around my monster girth. When she gives little whimpers of pain, I withdraw. I don't want to hurt my princess. Ever.

"Give it to me, Jason," she cries. "I want it all."

A growl breaks out of my throat, and I *let go*. I plunge myself deep into her pussy. She cries and clings to me, until I hit home. I'm balls-deep inside her. Her pussy is clamped around the base of my dick and it feels hot and torn. I've got her virginity. She's mine now. Forever. For a while, I hold still, absorbing this beautiful moment.

When I start to move inside her, she gives a shuddering sigh.

"Fuck, that feels good," she whispers.

That's all I need to hear. I pull out a little, then I thrust into her.

Again, and again and again.

"Oh... my god," she cries. "Jason, don't stop... Jason."

I close my eyes as ecstasy pours through me. I've heard my name shouted so many times over the years. By directors, by fans. But this is different. My mate, screaming out my name as I drive her wild. This is the only voice I've ever wanted to hear.

"Jason, I'm gonna..." Her soft thighs are wrapped around my hips, her nails are raking my back, and she explodes. She throws back her head and screams as my monster dick plunges into her virgin pussy over and over. I feel her tiny muscles clamping down around me, spasming, tighter and tighter. Holy hell, she's coming again... and again, all over my cock. It's like she's milking me, and I can't hold back. I lean back, flip her legs to the side, then without pulling out of her, I turn her right onto her front. I take in the sight of her little pink rosebud, of my cock disappearing between her cheeks, and I arch over her, my beast's canines breaking through my jaws.

As my climax approaches, I dip my head to the back of her neck.

She gives a squeal of pain, but holds still, like she's been waiting for this moment all along. My teeth break through her tender skin at the same instant that my cum bursts from the end of my dick. I feel it flood her little pussy like a firehose, filling her womb with my fertile seed.

I've marked her, filled her with my cum.

Mine! my beast roars.

Warmth and love pour through me as I pull out real slow and cradle her in my arms.

I've taken my mate.

9

Callie

The next morning, I wake up in Jason Trentino's bed. I still have no idea what that means to the rest of the world, and I don't care. All I know is he's the most amazing guy I've ever met, and I've fallen hard.

And now he's my mate.

I say the word over and over in my head.

Is it really possible?

So much happened yesterday. It was like months, or even years were contained within the span of a single day. My life went into overdrive in a big way. Yesterday morning I was a virgin who'd never even been kissed. And now…

Tingles go through me at the thought of everything we did yesterday. So many firsts.

My first ever kiss.

The first time I've seen a guy naked. And the first time anyone's ever seen me naked.

First orgasm.

First blow job.

Then his cock so deep inside me.

So big and thick.

The only one I'll ever want.

After he took my virginity yesterday, we fell asleep in each other's arms. Then we got up, showered, had dinner, and did it all again. In all those positions, that I didn't even know existed.

I have no idea what time it was when we finally fell asleep for the night, his huge muscular body cradling me, protecting me.

Now, his side of the bed is empty. Guess he got up already. I've got a feeling it's real late.

I look for my phone. It's here on the nightstand. And it's pulsating with seven new messages. All from Lindsay.

I groan then flick through them.

They're all okay. They all got picked up by the emergency services.

Ashley's leg is in a cast, and Lindsay has a sprain, but she's walking with crutches.

They all want to know if they can have their phones back and they promise not to mention anything of what happened yesterday to anyone. *Yada... yada.*

Then:

RU ok?

Just tell me one thing, are you and Jay-T like together?

Please tell me. I'll keep it a secret.

But if you give me an exclusive, I'll share the payment with you

Could be $$$$!

Please callie, this will really help my career

Id do the same for you

I snort out a laugh. Like hell she would. Then I tap out a message:

Linz, I love you because you're my sister. But you don't have an altruistic bone in your body. Let's be real about that.

Also, are you kidding me??? After the bear and me saved your life yesterday???

I dump my phone on the nightstand and get out of bed. I cast around for something to wear. My hiking gear is lying in a heap on the floor. It's probably all muddy and gross. Not very appealing. But there's a shirt, hanging over the back of a chair. I pick it up and instinctively press it to my face. It smells of fresh laundry, and *him*. Hope he won't mind me borrowing it. I pull it over my head, and it goes down to my knees.

My phone pings again:

Altru-whatever. You don't understand Callie. He's dangerous. I'm worried about you being alone with him.

Then she's calling me. I hit cancel.

"Dangerous, huh?" I look around for my underwear.

There's another ping.

Fine, if you won't answer my call, at least watch this!!!:

There's a link from YouTube.

I toss the phone on the bed in annoyance, but somehow I must've touched the play button, and the video starts up.

There's a bunch of soundbites from different news anchors, coming one after the other, like bullets:

"Trentino's promising career ends in shame."

"Jason Trentino seriously injures co-star on set."

"Trentino assault charge mysteriously 'disappears'… and so does Trentino."

"Jay T goes AWOL with career in tatters."

I grab the phone. There, on the screen, is Jason. But not as I know him. His hair is shorter and his beard is shaved off. He's bare-chested and wearing some kind of warrior outfit, and he's in the midst of what looks like a film set of ancient Rome… and he's going after some guy.

His fist is raised and he looks as mad as hell. The other guy has his hands raised in self-defense, but it looks like Jason is about to beat the crap out of him.

My heart lurching, I stab at the screen. I've seen enough.

Then something catches my eye: the golden statue sitting on a shelf in a corner of the room. I was wondering why it looked so familiar.

Because it's not a statue, doofus! It's a trophy. A famous actor's trophy.

Jason Trentino is a famous actor. An A-lister.

"But you knew that already, didn't you?" I mutter to myself.

I just didn't want to accept it, because I wanted so badly to believe he was my mate.

He's not my mate, because he's a big deal. A Hollywood star.

And soon he'll go back to his A-List life.

Last night was just a beautiful dream.

And if you don't want to end up with your heart broken, that's how you'll remember it.

But it's too late, because the truth is, I've fallen for him already. And the thought of being apart from him hurts my heart—

Bang!

There's a sound like a door smashing back against a wall.

Without stopping to think, I head out of the bedroom, and down the corridor to the living room.

Jason is not there, or in the kitchen. But the front door is swinging open.

I run to it and stare out at the wilderness. A cold, lonely breeze is blowing into the cabin, but there's no sign of him.

He's left me here.

Guess he realized yesterday was a mistake and he wants to get away from me.

* * *

Jason

MY BEAR IS TEARING through the forest, out of control. It bust out of me in an uncontrolled shift, and now it's snorting and foaming at the mouth.

But the blood running through my veins feels like ice. That darn video. What I would give to have it disappear from the Internet. My agent tried to have it taken down, but it keeps popping up, again and again.

I wanted to be the one to tell her. I was planning to take her in my arms and explain it all. After yesterday, I wasn't worried that she'd look me up and find that awful thing.

Fuck, fuck, fuck! My beast tips back its head and bellows out its pain into the trees.

She was deeply asleep when I left her, and I'd almost finished preparing her breakfast. Never occurred to me she'd wake up and start googling.

She doesn't trust me. That must be it. She must've seen something, or maybe I said something that made her doubt me. And now she's gonna hate my guts.

My beast runs on and on, churning up the ground with its lethal claws.

I wasn't planning to charge into the wilderness, but it freaked out. It couldn't stand the thought that I was going to lose her.

Stop, goddamnit! Finally, I get ahold of it. Its claws dig into the earth and it stands still, trembling and snorting.

She's my mate, and she trusts me. I know it, deep in my bones.

Someone must've sent her the video. That's the only thing that makes sense. And I don't have to scour my thoughts to figure out who that might be.

I rip a one-eighty and run hell for leather back to the cabin.

* * *

I'M STILL a hundred yards away when I see that the front door is wide open.

Was it me who left it that way?

I guess I must've.

But what's that, off to the side? I peer through the dense pines. Something white, fluttering in the breeze. My heart pounds.

I close up the distance in seconds. Soon, I'm sprinting up the stairs to the deck, and there she is, hanging over the wooden rail, gazing wistfully at the forest, wearing nothing but a white shirt. My shirt. When she catches sight of me, she gasps and presses her hand to her chest. Her eyes dart over my beastly features.

Then she relaxes.

She recognizes me. Relief pours through me.

I lower my massive head and slink over to her. And glory of glories, she reaches out her hands and lays them either side of my face, then she plants a kiss on my nose.

"I'd know you anywhere," she says. Her words pour through my veins like honey.

My beast lets out a long purr. She's my mate. Of course, she would.

Then she straightens up. "But now I want to see you as a man, Jason."

There's a hint of sternness in her voice which sends an electric charge right through me.

When I force my animal back down inside me, my cock is already at half-mast. I slap it down, drag her into my arms instead.

I hold her tight, feeling her trembling all over. When I pull back at last, her eyes are unnaturally bright.

"You're a famous actor," she says.

I let out a sigh. "I... I was. I'm sorry you had to see that video."

She shakes her head. "I turned it off as soon as I realized what it was. I don't care about the video, Jason."

"I owe you an explanation."

"You don't." She looks sad.

"I need to tell you, Callie."

"Okay." She gives herself a tiny shake. "I'm listening."

"The video that you saw, that everyone saw, makes me look like a psychopath, I know that. It wrecked my career. But there's more." I dart inside and grab my phone.

Then I start up the full video, the one that only I have access to, and show it to her.

When it ends, her eyes are full of tears. "That guy would've raped the girl if you hadn't intervened."

"Yup. He was the director, and she was an actress trying to get her first big break."

"Jason! you should've told everyone the truth," she exclaims.

"I don't think the director will prey on vulnerable women anymore. And the actress's career is going well." I shrug. "That's not all, though. The truth is, my beast was out of control. Turning feral. Directors liked me for these meathead roles, but I could hardly keep it inside me on set. It was just a matter of time before it really hurt someone."

She blinks. "Why was it like that?"

"Because I hadn't found my mate. It was getting real antsy. Happens with shifters sometimes. That's the *other* reason why I've been hiding out here in the wilderness."

"But that's so sad. You lost everything."

"Not everything." I reach for her, but she pulls away.

"Yesterday was just a… a thing, wasn't it?"

I shake my head, uncomprehending.

"It was a perfect, perfect day. But I wish you hadn't let me think we could be together." Her voice drags with regret.

I shake my head some more. "What do you mean? We are together. You're my mate."

"You're a famous, larger-than-life actor and I'm just an average chick. You should be with a supermodel or something."

I stare at her. Her words are like a knife in my gut.

"Nothing about you is average, Callie. You're the most amazing person I've met in my life. You're my mate. My only mate. There's never been anyone else. Ever."

Her beautiful lips part. "What do you mean?"

I shrug. "A shifter only mates with his mate."

Her eyes widen as she understands the implication of my words.

"Your pussy was the first to clench around my cock. Your womb was the first to be flooded with my seed."

"B-but you're so hot, and…and you must've had women all over you."

I shake my head. "Shifters aren't like human guys. That kind of crap means nothing to us." I grab the neck of her shirt and pull it down, exposing the mark I gave her last night. It's beautiful; a deep shade of reddish purple, like a stormy sunset. "Did you forget about this?"

She puts her hand to it. "It tingles. I mean, it was tingling like crazy a minute ago."

"That's because we were apart," I tell her. "Our souls are connected. They always were—via some invisible thread that joined us. But now we've mated, the bond is so much more powerful."

She blushes. "I thought it was like a love bite or something. I mean, I knew it wasn't, but I could hardly believe it."

I suppress a grin. "Nothing like a love bite. This here, means you're mine. Forever."

Her lovely hazel eyes lock onto mine. "Forever," she repeats.

"I love you, Callie."

"Oh, I love you, too."

My heart booming, I sweep her up into my arms, and I kiss her long and deep. When I perch her sweet ass on the porch rail and slide between her thighs, I discover she's not wearing anything under my shirt. And her hot little pussy is at the perfect height to press against my swollen cock.

Holy hell, she's wet already. When I slide my cock up and down her pretty lips, she moans into my mouth, and her soft hands clutch at my shoulders. Naturally, my cock slides into her entrance.

I feel her tense. "Easy, baby," I mutter, and I guide my broad head into her. She's not a virgin anymore, and my shaft goes in easier. I feel her tiny muscles gripping me tight as she opens for me.

"Oh, my god," she whispers as I thrust in, more and more of my dick filling her tiny pussy. When I hit home, she gasps. I've impaled her with my monster cock. Her lips are red and parted and her eyes are a little glassy.

And I need to see more of her. I tear open the buttons of my shirt and yank it off her shoulders, releasing her lovely big tits. There she is, as nature intended. A beautiful, naked goddess. The two of us outside, in the wilderness. I kiss her deep as I rut into her, squeezing her soft tits. When I fuck her harder, she tips her head back and lets out wild cries, her voice echoing through the trees. She's so wet, so slippery. I feel her clench tighter and tighter, then she starts to come all over my cock. Spasming around me, while one orgasm after another rips through her. Her fingernails are sharp on my back, and I fucking love it. She's not a little rabbit; she's my wild she-bear.

I thrust and thrust. I'm gonna breed her. I'm gonna fill her belly with my cubs, and we're going to have a big, noisy, happy house, full of little shifters that are as sweet and tough as their mama. And I don't give a damn about anybody else. Let them gawk and click their dumb camera phones. All that matters is right here—Callie and me.

EPILOGUE

Four months later

"*R*eady to rock and roll?" Monica asks.

I take a deep breath. "Ready as I'll ever be."

"You look so beautiful, Callie. Like a fairy princess."

When I turn to her, her eyes are shining with tears.

"Stop, you'll set me off, too." I laugh, hugging her. She's been so happy for me, so supportive. And she looks stunning in her emerald-green bridesmaid's dress, which sets off her flame-red hair and her curves. I can't wait for her to find her own mate.

I pull my dress tight against my stomach. "Am I showing?"

"You sure are!"

I cradle my bump. I'm so happy and proud that I'll be walking down the aisle with Jason's cub in my belly.

Monica peeks between the dressing-room curtains. A little *ooh* of surprise bursts from her lips.

"There are a ton of famous people out there, aren't there?"

"Yup!" Her voice comes out as a squeak.

"Oh, god." My stomach does a little flip. "Guess it's lucky that I won't recognize most of them."

"Well, none of them are as cool or as beautiful as you." She re-curls a ringlet of my hair. "And none of them are marrying the best guy in the world."

"Thanks, Mon," I say, adjusting the shoulder strap of her dress. "You're a sweetheart." And I smile. The old me would've thrown her compliment right back in her face.

"It's all true…" Her eyes get that glazed look she has when an idea occurs to her. "You remember that mantra that was supposed to get you through the camping trip?"

"It's just three days? How could I forget?"

"Turned out it was a whole lot more than that."

"It sure was," I say, meeting her eyes in the mirror.

"You deserve all the happiness in the world, Callie."

"So do you, Mon." I take another big breath. "Okay, think I'm ready."

Monica peeks through the curtain again and signals the usher. A moment later, the music starts up. She takes my arm, and the curtains open.

Honestly, all I see is a sea of blurry faces as I walk down the aisle. Monica is my only bridesmaid, and she's also giving me away. She's always been my entire family, so of course she's the one I want at my side. And, it doesn't hurt to give her a little exposure at the wedding, with so many eligible bachelors around, and all.

Everything goes into slow motion as Jason steps out from his seat and turns to face me. My breath catches. His huge, muscular body is encased in a tux, and he looks absolutely incredible. He's trimmed his beard and his big, soft eyes are brighter than ever as he takes me in. He holds his hands out to me, and there's a big *ooh!* From the guests. It might not be traditional, but neither of us give a damn. All that matters is our love for each other, and this cub I'm carrying. There's been plenty of gossip about our "shotgun wedding", as Lindsay has been telling me gleefully. But the truth is that Jason made me pregnant the night he claimed me, and that's what counts. This wedding is partly for his family. They're so proud of him and his glittering career. When I first met them, I was worried they'd be disappointed that he was marrying a civilian like me, instead of a famous actress. But they're shifters, of course, so they're ecstatic that he's found his fated mate, and I get on real well with Jason's mom, dad and younger brother.

The wedding is also designed to silence all the speculation about him. That was my idea. He says he doesn't want to go back into acting. But I've seen all his movies now, and I've been telling him it's not fair to deprive the public of his talent and godlike presence.

I've also granted Lindsay an exclusive wedding photoshoot. After all, she's done me a solid. If she hadn't decided to spend her bachelorette party trying to expose Jason, he and I might never have met.

When I approach Jason and slide my hands into his,

the love shining in his eyes turns my knees weak. "You look so, so beautiful, my little She-bear," he says. Except he doesn't say it out loud. His soul speaks directly to mine, and I feel his words in my chest.

"Thank you," I whisper, and break into a grin. She-bear is his nickname for me, mostly when we're mating. Because I'm so wild, apparently.

The ceremony is a blur. We make the promises to each other that we've already made in private, then there's clapping and cheering and a million camera flashes. Then lots of hugs and congratulations.

The two shifters who rescued Lindsay and Ashley are Jason's best men. We've spent a lot of time hanging out together in the past few months, and Logan and Caleb are both great guys.

Everyone wants to talk to me, it seems. Guess they all want to find out who Jay T's shotgun bride is. It's actually kinda fun. I'm deep in conversation with a young actress who's just been nominated for an Oscar, when Jason pulls me aside.

"Callie, I need to borrow you for a minute," he says urgently.

"Sure thing." I tell the actress I'll catch her later, and the next thing I know, he's hurrying me through the venue, which is a beautiful old French chateau. He pulls me into a small dressing room and locks the door behind us.

"Where's the fire?" I say, looking around confusedly.

"Right here." He takes my hand and presses it to his crotch.

"Ohh..." I say. His cock is already hard.

"You're so sexy, Callie. I couldn't wait any longer," he growls.

Then I'm in his arms, and he's kissing me hungrily, tracing his burning lips all over my neck and cleavage. There's a zip that runs all the way down the back of my dress. His fingers find it and tug it down. He peels the whole dress off, and his eyes sear over me from head to toe. I'm wearing bridal lingerie—bra, panties, stockings and a garter belt—the whole deal. Makes a weird contrast with my big, round, pregnant belly, but if the tent in Jason's pants is anything to go by, he likes what he sees.

"Gorgeous pregnant mama," he says, his voice thick with need.

When he slips a hand into my satin panties, I'm already soaking wet.

"These are coming off," he growls. He crouches down to slide them down my thighs, and suddenly, his tongue is on my clit.

And he doesn't quit until my legs tremble and I clamp my lips together to stop myself from screaming.

Then he leans me over a dressing table and he's entering me from behind. He rocks into me, working my clit with his fingers. He's gentler these days as my baby bump grows, worried he'll hurt me or our little one. The baby books say it's fine, but I love this new softness in him. He's gonna be such a great dad. I can't wait to see him with our cub in his arms for the first time.

As I come around his big pulsing cock, the rest of the world slips away—the guests, the cameras, the lavish celebrations—and it's just me and my big, sexy bear mate.

"We'd better get back," I say, a few minutes later. Jason is holding me tight, face buried in the side of my neck, while the final waves of our orgasms fade away.

He gives a groan. "Guess you're right."

I twist around in his arms and kiss him one more time. "We've got all night, you know."

"We sure have," he growls, stroking my cheek with his callused fingertips.

For our honeymoon, he's booked us into a cabin deep in the French wilderness. It has a retractable roof, so we can make love under the stars. We're both looking forward to centering ourselves after these hectic few months. I love our new fast-paced life, but the most special times for us will always be out in nature, remembering how a famous, reclusive grizzly shifter met his little human mate.

THE END

READ THE OTHER BOOKS IN THE SERIES

If you like fated-mate romances, with plenty of V-card fun and tons of feels, check out the other books in the series at:

arianahawkes.com/obsessed-mountain-mates

READ MY OTHER OBSESSED MATES SERIES

If you like steamy insta-love romance, featuring obsessed, growly heroes who'll do anything for their mates, check out my Obsessed Mates series. All books are standalone and can be read in any order.

Get started at arianahawkes.com/obsessed-mates

READ THE REST OF MY CATALOGUE

MateMatch Outcasts: a matchmaking agency for beasts, and the women tough enough to love them.

★★★★★ "A super **exciting, funny, thrilling, suspenseful and steamy shifter romance series**. The characters jump right off the page!"

★★★★★ "**Absolutely Freaking Fantastic**. I loved every single word of this story. It is so full of **exciting twists that will keep you guessing until the very end** of this book. I can't wait to see what might happen next in this series."

Ragtown is a small former ghost town in the mountains, populated by outcast shifters. It's a secretive place, closed-off to the outside world - until someone sets up a secret mail-order bride service that introduces women looking for their mates.

Get started at arianahawkes.com/matematch-outcasts

MY OTHER MATCHMAKING SERIES

My bestselling *Shiftr: Swipe Left For Love* series features Shiftr, the secret dating app that brings curvy girls and sexy shifters their perfect match! Fifteen books of totally bingeworthy reading — and my readers tell me that Shiftr is their favorite app ever! ;-) Get started at arianahawkes. com/shiftr

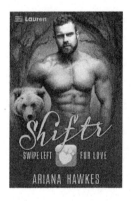

★★★★★ **"Shiftr is one of my all-time favorite series**! The stories are funny, sweet, exciting, and scorching hot! And they will **keep you glued to the pages**!"

★★★★★ **"I wish I had access to this app**! Come on, someone download it for me!"

Get started at arianahawkes.com/shiftr

CONNECT WITH ME

If you'd like to be notified about new releases, giveaways and special promotions, you can sign up to my mailing list at arianahawkes.com/mailinglist. You can also follow me on BookBub and Amazon at:

bookbub.com/authors/ariana-hawkes
amazon.com/author/arianahawkes

Thanks again for reading – and for all your support!

Yours,
Ariana

* * *

USA Today bestselling author Ariana Hawkes writes spicy romantic stories with lovable characters, plenty of suspense, and a whole lot of laughs. She told her first story at the age of four, and has been writing ever since, for both work and pleasure. She lives in Massachusetts with her husband and two huskies.

www.arianahawkes.com

GET TWO FREE BOOKS

Join my mailing list and get two free books.

Once Bitten Twice Smitten

A 4.5-star rated, comedy romance featuring one kickass roller derby chick, two scorching-hot Alphas, and the naughty nip that changed their lives forever.

Lost To The Bear

He can't remember who he is. Until he meets the woman he'll never forget.

Get your free books at arianahawkes.com/freebook

READING GUIDE TO ALL OF MY BOOKS

Obsessed Mates

Her River God Wolf

Her Biker Wolf

Her Alpha Neighbor Wolf

Her Bad Boy Trucker Wolf

Her Second Chance Wolf

Her Convict Wolf

Obsessed Mountain Mates

Driven Wild By The Grizzly

Snowed In With The Grizzly

Chosen By The Grizzly

Shifter Dating App Romances

Shiftr: Swipe Left for Love 1: Lauren

Shiftr: Swipe Left for Love 2: Dina

Shiftr: Swipe Left for Love 3: Kristin

Shiftr: Swipe Left for Love 4: Melissa

Shiftr: Swipe Left for Love 5: Andrea

Shiftr: Swipe Left for Love 6: Lori

Shiftr: Swipe Left for Love 7: Adaira

Shiftr: Swipe Left for Love 8: Timo

Shiftr: Swipe Left for Love 9: Jessica

Shifter Holiday Romances

Bear My Holiday Hero

Ultimate Bear Christmas Magic Boxed Set Vol. 1

Ultimate Bear Christmas Magic Boxed Set Vol. 2

Printed in Great Britain
by Amazon

27621970R00059